STREET FIRE

BY DANIEL HALPERN

Street Fire 1975
The Lady Knife-Thrower 1974
The Songs of Mririda
  (with Paula Paley) 1974

Borges on Writing (with
  Norman Thomas di Giovanni
  and Frank MacShane) 1973
Traveling on Credit 1972

STREET FIRE

DANIEL HALPERN

The Viking Press New York

First published in 1975 by The Viking Press, Inc.
625 Madison Avenue, New York, N.Y. 10022
Published simultaneously in Canada by
The Macmillan Company of Canada Limited

LIBRARY OF CONGRESS CATALOGING IN PUBLICATION DATA
Halpern, Daniel.
  Street fire.

  Poems.
  I. Title.
PS3558.A397S7   811'.5'4   74-34025
ISBN 0-670-67815-5

Printed in U.S.A.

ACKNOWLEDGMENTS | Grateful acknowledgment is made to the following
magazines, in which these poems were first published.
"For One Who Has Understood Little," *Sewanee Review*, 82 (fall 1974),
copyright by the University of the South, and reprinted by permission of
the editor. | *American Poetry Review*: "Clove As Ego," "The Breaker of
Glass." | *Antaeus*: "Déja Vu," "Summer 1970." | *Atlantic Monthly*: "The
New Blast Furnace at the Kemerovo Metallurgical Combine." | *Boundary
2*: "The Landing." | *The Carleton Miscellany*: "Pig." | *Esquire*: "The
Gathering," "There," "Street Fire," "Brandy Cat." | *Goddard Journal*:
"The Midnight Caller," "The Wind at Tabelbala." | *Harper's*: "The
Whippet Ball." | *Jeopardy*: "Objects." | *The Nation*: "Rituals," "God
Hasn't Made Room." | *New York Quarterly*: "Church in Midsummer." |
The New York Review of Books: "Silence." | *The New Yorker*: "The Lady
Knife-Thrower." | *The North American Review*: "The Domestic Cliché
of Love." | *Northwest Review*: "The Girl Who Doesn't Smile." | *Ohio
Review*: "Rubber Junction." | *Paintbrush*: "The Sisterhood." | *Prairie
Schooner*: "Before the Meal." | *A Review*: "The Soldier." | *The Southern
Review*: "Endings," "Fever Journal," "Nebraskan Childhood." | *Translation
74*: "The Insult," "To the Skouris and the Rats."
The author would like also to thank the following presses, which published
some of the poems in this collection: *Barlenmir House, The Bellevue Press,
The Unicorn Press*.
The translations of Mririda n'Ait Attik's poems were done with Paula Paley.
Thanks also goes to the National Endowment for the Arts, for grants in
1973–1974, and 1974–1975.

FOR CAROL

CONTENTS

I

THE LANDING

II

THE OTHER

|||

TRANSLATIONS
Poems by
Bella Akhmadulina
and
Mririda n'Aït Attik

|V

THE GATHERING

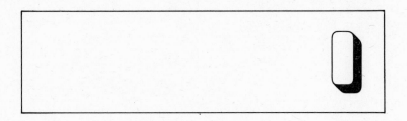

THE LANDING

STREET FIRE

FOR *Chico*

It is past midnight in a thick fog when sirens
call us to the terrace.
We look down onto blossoms of bright fire
opening from manholes on Fifth Avenue.
There are men standing and smoking in rubber jackets
outside a garment-district café,
the lights fluttering, the fire
offering us its electric smoke.
In bare feet and robes—the cat
and dog at our feet—we hear
the heat pound tubes stuffed with wire.
And somewhere down there, under the softening blacktop,
the gas mains wait to take in the whole block.
We bring the two or three small relics of our lives,
the dog and cat, and the elevator to the street.
There is a cold wind and ice in the gutters.
There is the street's midnight population
leaning against the wall of Reverend Peale's Sunday Church.
We note the taxis that deliver strangers
to watch with us as the street shrivels and begins
to flow around the manhole covers.
They are all there: men of the brigade, the police,
women from nearby hotels, their furred men,
the strangers from the city.

What we see is the tip of the iceberg,
they tell us—and underneath
the tubes alive with flames.
For an hour we watch from the corner—
in this weather tragedies are distant.
The elevator back up contains the momentary explosion
in the eye where disasters flare—
our section of New York, between the flowers and furs,
is full of bright red petals.
We reach the ninth floor and step into air
powdered with radiator heat.
The tiny, muffled beats of fire below the street
pant through the window an even pulse.
The dog moves into the living room where the fire is dying
on bricks. The cat takes the warm tiles
of the bathroom. We stand silently, listen
a few minutes, then move to each other.
Our own fire is watered by the conviction
that things are right. Later, we listen to the small puffs
of heat spit from the manholes outside, smell
the smoke from live wires
bound with rubber that smolders into morning.

RUBBER JUNCTION

I am a man who has watched the sun break down
upon the single mountain of our plain.
There are sparrows in the air, nothing more
save the dust of ten generations.

In the morning I collect wood for the fire.
In the afternoon the train arrives on time.
In the evening, on the long porch, I fill my pipe,
letting the blue smoke out evenly into the pink

light leaning into the shadows around the house.
The children here grow up and train out before
understanding the imperceptible finger
of time that tamps year into year,

the train with its faces, legs of centipedes crawling
through the sand, around our single mountain.
There is little, really, to say—
the dreams of the dead will take us in their hands

and shake us into a sleep of their own.
I know it is something not unknown to me
I see, watching the sun break down
behind the single mountain of our plain.

Perhaps one day, while I am collecting wood in the morning,
a dark cloud will spread itself on top of my armful of wood,
and I'll carry it, unsuspecting, into the house.
Later, when we've touched the roots of night,

lightning will burst through the halls,
thunder sounding through the bedrooms,
bringing us to our sleeping feet
as the flood begins a slow descent down the stairs.

THE LANDING

*Out here a woman wonders.
And if she has no man
her arms get strong.*
— CAROLYN FORCHÉ

On the prow,
standing on red planks,
the white maiden holds
hand to temple,
faint, keening.
The fog snags the edge
of her gown, dissolves
it at the ankle, begins
for thighs, for breasts
unlike white stone, her
neck, and then her
lips like white stone.
She sees scrub, dabbed
on a mountain, its peak
thrust through the layer of air-cloth.
There are sirens of anger in the air
that call to trees.
Wasps prowl the reef—
the maiden, kneeling now,
watches them,
watches parrot fish bite and snap
for food, lovers
of the vegetable, hanging in kelp beds.
And now, behind her,

behind wasp and siren,
the ship of women prisoners
begins to undo itself.
The fog,
the life's-breath in a cold
climate, lifts.
Their legs are thin and hard
from the voyage, they are wise
progeny of the white maiden
who moves their vessel
past wasps who have given way,
past parrot fish in kelp
with their bright colors
less brilliant than hers,
and onto the wave that rises,
lifts them, lifts them up
level with mountain scrub,
then down
through layers of water,
down to the soft fingers of sand
that are not their fathers
and yet,
and yet take them in.

THE SISTERHOOD

If you let them, they'll take your eyes away,
knock out the sight-spot inside the color

on a stone and carry them off, blind, to the street
where they come from. They'll polish those balls

on rugs and wear them between their fine shoulders.
If they could see, they'd see you walking downtown

with a white stick or a dog. Your hands now are sockets.
Your arms thin chains hanging beyond the seat of your hips.

If you relax with sun-heat in your mouth near night,
they'll come up behind you and carry away your tongue.

You might have told them it didn't speak,
but now it's too late. They take it to their street

where they rub it down with the domestic oils
from their bodies. They're not glad to have it

when they discover it won't talk. They beat it
with the fiction of their mouths and bury it.

When the tongue, thick with the weight of earth
lifts into flower, it sings to your teeth

from the garden where they live.
You can hear it, but nothing more.

You didn't let them take your eyes away.
They stole your tongue that didn't speak

and beat it and buried it and wore your eyes.
The eyes are blind. You hear them clicking

on their chains outside your door.
You guess that the rest is easy.

They unsheathe the knives of your fantasy.
They begin the long incision into sleep—

the blade runs for the eyes of your dream,
lifts you upon its edge to the waking street.

THE OTHER

All clowns are masked and all
  personae
Flow from choices; sad and gay,
  wise,
Moody and humorous are chosen
  faces,
And yet not so! For all are
  circumstances,
Given, like a tendency
To colds or like blond hair and
  wealth,
Or war and peace or gifts for
  mathematics,
Fall from the sky, rise from the
  ground, stick to us
In time, surround us. . . .
— DELMORE SCHWARTZ

DÉJÀ VU

The great wings of the fan spread
the air around the bed, the cat
pads through the hall after errant sound.

I awake in a fist of pale light
to touch you awake. I am dreaming
this moment that years from now

another will share
as he sits up in bed
next to you

and in your sleeping face
know that he has been here once,
but in another room—

he hears the swish
of an overhead fan and the cat
as it leaps for the sound

that brought him out of sleep.
When he touches you
it will be with my hands.

THE LADY KNIFE-THROWER

FOR *Sandy*

In the gay, silver air of the tent
I'm at ease, fingers
at rest in my lap.
Before me the tools of my trade—
cleaned, well oiled and waiting
for the warmth of my hand, for the time
when the flick of my wrist will send them
out into the morning for their casual trip
to my husband's waiting body.
One at a time they plant themselves at his sides,
tucking in the air around his body.

At night, under the big top,
he is strapped to the board.
With a roll of drums I appear with my knives
and release my repertoire of throws.

There is no question in our lives of fidelity.
At night, after the knives are cleaned and placed
in their teakwood rack, we are all we desire.

THE BREAKER OF GLASS

for *Moira*

It pleases him, how he multiplies
in the pool of glass he leaves
after his tiny hammer touches
telephone booths, lights of cars and windows.
He can feel himself freeze into pattern,
fall to pieces on the ground.
He hates what he breaks,
the smooth run of it on air.

Some men go for young girls,
the knuckles they've grown under their sweaters.
Others watch buildings fold up in flames.
He loves the pool of glass,
the cool sense of escape.
When the glass he's after is gone
he returns to his stone house,
lays the hammer on wood,
and looks deeply for himself
in the bathroom's dark wall.

THE MIDNIGHT CALLER

I'm the guy who calls you
when you're slipping into dream,
who drops the bell onto the acrobats
of sleep to touch you through wire.

I'll ask after your sleeping attire,
your hair, crushed thyme in your thighs.
I'll hit you up for the act of darkness
and groan till you're primped and wet.

Don't hang up! You can't trace this one—
I reach through sound, please for a dime
if you'll loosen a little. My dear!
Your fingers! The smile at your waist!

PIG

It is on a late afternoon—
the tide moving in three directions,
the ocean, a bottle-green quilt of nimbus—
that one of the pigs slides
into the Atlantic. The wind carries us on
with the steady purr of the prop.
The pig, held by fat in the wake,
not swimming, not sinking,
lets its pig eyes dance
to us as the water stops churning
and the boat moves away.

*

There is no sound in the rubber air.
The tide moves south, like birds,
warm, rich with fish.

Somewhere, three days off the coast of America,
the air is silent.
I can hear nothing, being too far out for birds.
There is only the soft, warm slapping
of the tide that carries me.
My eyes, wild bees in the silence, moving south.

RITUALS

Yes, I've taken to checking the lock
    more than once before sleeping.
The gas jets too get tested.
    You might say it's my way.
You might guess that I wash my hands
    a little too often
and count a lot.
    My doctor says counting is normal.
We all have things to count,
    I count what I'm not sure of.
My repetitions are defensive,
    they give me something to do.
Think of it as magic:
    I count to five
I assure the safety of five
    members of my family. Simple!
What would I do if I didn't
    count?
I might take an edge to someone's features,
    who knows?
But everything is as it should be:
    what I love I hate:
I love what moves away,

or lingers outside my door.
I count minutes when I'm not sure,
    but never people,
they can turn on you.
    With numbers it's different.
You can count on them.

OBJECTS

*Two silver figures reported walk-
ing on a road outside Xenia,
Ohio, thought to be from outer
space.*   — AP

In our mint-green Buick my wife
and I are driving to Xenia
out of Mutual, Ohio.
On the shoulder of the road
two silver figures are walking.
We continue on.
In our rearview mirror
we're dazzled by the flash
of sun off their expensive bodies,
their stiff gait along the road.

We watch the fields tilt, the clumps of cumulus
turn camel, turn elephant, turn cat,
the figures now dimes in the distance.

In Xenia we give our story of the silver figures.
In the morning we read
of the couple tailored in tinfoil.

Really something, we think,
back in our mint-green Buick,
driving the golden forehead of Ohio,
below the sapphire kingdom of sky.

ENGAGEMENT

He meets me for dinner with manners.
All right, age spreads like a lung
to encompass every other breathing thing.
Mild as a Millie I once knew, I cut
through the tenderloin while his knees
part mine like butter. His tie
is of an exquisite blue. Silver
cufflinks charm my sleeve as he pins
me to the table. Now biscuits
warm as what waits below the table,
taped to the waist like a vial.
I'm content to let the wine span
our difference. He at fifty
goes off sweet at the tongue
after minced lamb. As mint
jelly tags his cuff, I fall for him.

Once my father bent to me, his weight
part of mine: strange,
now this man weighs on me. His knee
moves past respect—my age,
my lack of age. . . . I watch him count
the tip into the check. At midnight,
before the lights, he lifts me

through an elderly romance. His fire
is a little less than pleasing, fanned
by his own lack of breath. Love
he says is a green apple pinned
to the brow of a cagey girl.

Cagey, I turn from sleep
and call a stranger.

OUR SAD BEASTS

Like nothing
they left their pants at the door
bras hung from chairs
I watched them
smoothly
rise bald for mates
Our sad beasts from their caves
hungered back
Slowly
first one then many
the eyes went out
One by one they disappeared
rocked somewhere from sound
The whole room danced
I put my head back
balancing in the rhythm
that beat time against the floor

THERE

They play with their hands here
for hours
afloat on fingers of boredom
Their smiles come in odd shapes
appear at strange intervals
The attendants are bleached
everything is pleasant
but stripped of anything pleasing
The letters from your own brittle world
click like plastic
We eat on plates that are almost rubber
the others will try anything
slice their features
with any sharp edge in reach
Everything here is soft but your flowers
were armed with a scent
that set the patients on edge
Remember how you told me
when you held me then before you left
that you were not the thief of my words
Our wounds will open their lips to each other
when the doors open
and I come through the padding
holding your name

TRANSLATIONS

Poems by
Bella Akhmadulina
and
Mririda n'Aït Attik

SILENCE

— BELLA AKHMADULINA

Who was it that took away my voice?
The black wound he left in my throat
can't even cry.

March is at work under the snow
and the birds of my throat are dead,
their gardens turning into dictionaries.

I beg my lips to sing.
I beg the lips of the snowfall,
of the cliff and the bush to sing.

Between my lips, the round shape
of the air in my mouth.
Because I can say nothing,

I'll try anything
for the trees in the snow.
I breathe. I swing my arms. I lie.

From this sudden silence,
like death, that loved
the names of all words,
you raise me now in song.

THE NEW BLAST-FURNACE IN THE
KEMEROVO METALLURGICAL COMBINE

— BELLA AKHMADULINA

Up there where the new blast-furnace rises
they are working.
A boy is laughing
as he balances in the wind.

Indifferently, he walks the thin ledge
and for a moment, just slightly,
tilts his head as if yearning
for the ground that awaits him.

He is at ease in the echo
of his erratic footfall,
in the scatter of sparks like fistfuls
of failing stars in an August sky.

Of course there is the bravado,
the passion and sudden expectation
that a passing girl will understand
the distance, his height above ground.

Girls have other things in mind—
one will look up, see him, and understand
nothing. It is something farther
that calls to her, something beyond him.

And yet, on a rare trip to the circus,
she will strain forward, pale
with concern for the walker
when he steps onto the wire.

With his anger cloaked, and almost cool,
he again looks down
onto the girls who have left him,
then scatters sparks, failing stars of fire.

GOD HASN'T MADE ROOM

— MRIRIDA N'AÏT ATTIK

My sister, you are a stranger to this place.
Why be surprised that I know nothing?
My eyes have never seen the rose.
My eyes have never seen the orange.
They say there is plenty down there
in the good country
where people and animals and plants are never cold.
My sister, stranger from the plains,
don't laugh at a barefoot girl from the mountains
who dresses in coarse wool.
In our fields and pastures
God hasn't made room for the orange.
God hasn't made room for the rose.
I have never left my village and its nut trees.
I know only the arbutus berries and red hawthorn,
and the leaves of green basil
that keep the mosquitoes away
when I fall asleep on the terrace
on a warm summer night.

TO THE SKOURIS AND THE RATS

— MRIRIDA N'AÏT ATTIK

I told you, women of the house,
to the Skouris and the rats, don't open your door!

He came, Ba Allal, he came
with his daughter, the daughter of Ba Allal the Skouri.

And now, no day passes without her morning greeting,
her idle chatter at noon, her evening smile.

In truth, she came to ask for burning coals!
Yes, and she came to bring cakes and borrow the sifter!
And the mortar, without the pestle!
In truth, she lingered in the dark staircase,
where the master of the house often happened to be!
Yes, and she came to bring the mortar back
(it seems the pestle was somewhere in the staircase)!

She came back often, the daughter of the Skouri.
And then she stayed,
now the darling young wife of the master!

Didn't I tell you, women of the house?
To the Skouris and the rats, don't open your door!

THE INSULT

— MRIRIDA N'AÏT ATTIK

You are wrong, mother of my former husband,
if you think I am suffering.
You can tell your son who left me
that the good and bad days of our life together
are gone from my mind and heart,
just as straws scatter in the wind. . . .

I remember nothing of the work in the fields,
the loads that bruised my back,
the jugs that marked my shoulders,
my fingers, burned baking bread,
the bones he left me on festival days.

He took back the jewelry. Had he given it to me?
Did he beat me?
Did he take me in his arms?
I can't remember. . . .

It's as if I had never known him.

You who were my mother-in-law, go tell your son
that I no longer know his name!

THE GATHERING

THE WIND AT TABELBALA

> . . . *A quiet place when the wind*
> *is not blowing.*
> — PAUL BOWLES

The wind rises up out of the night
like something hostile. And then,
fades.

I finger your image
into a letter I've swept with sweet lines,
as I would you with hands
that jump from darkness
where night is nothing.

A great wind, my dear, throttles the night
and winter lurks on the very buildings
of this far city.

It's just now midnight
and the room leans toward the fire.
The pulse of an *oud*
races in the café below
with the blue smoke of good *kif*,

blown from its form
by wind.

I leave the room
(adding wood to the fire)
for tea and the *oud*.

One can hear wind on wires
articulating mood.

From your Western roost
try and think of mint tea for pennies,
and strange men,
heads in hoods of *djellabas,*
talking in a night tongue
harsh as the desert.

I turn the thought of you seeing me here,
hinged to my table over tea,
off.

Each window
in turn
bangs to a rhythm of the wind.

After posting your letter
I take a long way back,
through alleys like veins.
I find my room
the color of dying fire,

and as I nod in a chair toward morning,
the wind finds voice

to remind me the fire wants pumping,
and with winter on the walls
I am its constant slave.

FEVER JOURNAL

It is evening. Purple
smoke rises from the fields:
they are burning the clothing
of the infected and the dead,
those few without fever.
It is evening and I am sitting
with tea, reading in the yellow light.

Today is Sunday. No bells.
Only the unwinding of the muezzins
over the valley, down to the river.
The steady pulse of drums is gone.

I awake in the night,
the warm hands of fever

at my temples. I imagine
this, the head
taking over my body,
flapping it out on the bed
like laundry upon the river.
I hear dogs moving in the street,
frogs breathing under the bridge.
My hands are cool.
There is light in the window.
I have survived another night.

3 MARCH

This morning birds
flew out of the smoke
heading north across the water.
I remain here with the fever,
without mail, with radio reports
that carry the news of Europe.

1 APRIL

The first day of Ramadan.
Rats move against the sunset
on electric wires into the trees.
The burning continues, and I wait.

12 APRIL

Upon waking, I drink whiskey,
nap from noon till cannon's call.
I move to the dim light of a café.
There is little talk. The radio
blasts Egyptian film music.

27 APRIL

The smells of the marketplace
are lost. Smoke
is everywhere. Only a quick
trace of mint at afternoon tea.

5 MAY

Today the sun is bright
and it has ended.

We have been marked by the fever.

And now it is evening—
I watch the last of the smoke
rise to meet the birds, moving
back over the water from the north.

THE SOLDIER

A soldier is walking in the streets of a very old city.
The women wear veils. The men are unfriendly.
The sun is not hot but there is dust
in sheets between every building.
He kicks the dogs that feed on his heels.
He pushes past crowds of children
whose hands are hats of loose change.

In its descent a kite drops to his head,
leaving a thin red line.
He picks up a chicken from a pile of seeds
and throws it at a wall.
A passerby asks, What has this chicken done to you?
The soldier replies, By God, a brother of his
left this mark on my head.
Yes, answers the passerby, but this is a domestic
chicken, and that was a wild kite.
Never mind, said the soldier.
They are birds, both this and that.

He leaves behind the walls of the city,
the veiled women, the begging dogs and children.
He walks in air free of dust and sound.

By midday he knows there will be no water
as the sun leans for him—
a bright bird out of the cobalt, like all the others.

THE DOMESTIC CLICHÉ OF LOVE

In the brown basement
of the Turkish restaurant
the acrobat is on his hands
on a chair,
the juggler with the dinner's
supply of plates in the air,
the snake charmer
lip to tongue with his cobra.

You watch
feet in the air,
plates hand to hand
and the snake
complacent on the mouth
of another.

This is your life,
here in the brown basement
of my city—my feet
in the air, plates
at my fingertips,
the logical extension of the cobra's tongue
that gives you that final kiss
goodnight.

BEFORE THE MEAL

FOR *Marguerite*

Your favorite composer is on the organ.
    Your friend is against the west wall,
        against the fire, burning Moroccan wood.

Together we arrive in the rain, thyme
    jumps from the walk under our steps,
        the two of us moving for the door

of El Foolk on the Old Mountain,
    your black dress lifted off the rain.
        There are shells in the anteroom, dark

oils by McBey on pink walls, alive
    with flames that keep us, that place a finger
        against the mold moving in the corners.

One by one your guests are delivered by taxi.
    The servants are certain in their whites—
        tonic, *kif* for the native, Polish vodka

for those without English.
    There is the long fugue that fans the fire.
        In the vase, flowers give off that deadly scent.

CHURCH IN MIDSUMMER

On the ledge of a canal
leading back to San Marco
stone lions, humorous and mangy,
crouch before the church, a foot
from the still water.
Inside, cool marble air,
frankincense scoring the skeins
of blue light. The saints
of the wall darken year after year
and are restored. The air here
is from a hundred feet down,
or like the air in the tombs
near Karnak.
My friend buys candles to burn for us,
while in that secular dark another voice
strums where the church is richest. Latin
monotone: *basso buffo* or coloratura?
My friend is drowning
in lace and the lassitude
holiness brings to sinners.
The blue light scores the mood here. . . .
The Venetian sun beat the tourists
to church—the cool marble of air,
the blue light lying down.

SUMMER, 1970

FOR *B.*

Now, after a party with the consul and our best friend,
my mother, I walk back to your flat over the Arno
freckled with light, lined by a small wind
or frogs, and hold you in the air of your terrace.
Your black hair a wood scent and dark,
the thickness of pitch or dark amber—
an olfaction of night. We go inside
to comb your hair. You bring brandy, there is glass
on wood, our tongues on fire, the flames licking
the lonely caves of speech by day, together
here, moving quickly in silence. We are
silly in the brilliance, the giddy moon
eats your secret, the long upturning of nose
and breast (hydrangeas after water at sunset),
the wedge of light upon the couch
near brandy, and my mouth that calls you, calls you.

FOR ONE WHO HAS UNDERSTOOD LITTLE

Your eyes climb the trellis, settle in the paisley
patterns that net the greenery of your house.
I'm quick to flatter what's beneath the satin

that covers the movement of your body.
My hands carry you back to your parents'
eyes. . . . There was a field, turning

high and yellow, the odor of sleep. They lay
with grass to their chins and pressed you to them.
It took all this: the field unwinding, the heat

of a man, a woman's slow willingness
beneath him. . . . Their breathing understood
nothing of your name—it came to them

later, when their dark exhaustion held them.
Together, we watch our shadows, how they drift
on the wall, climb for darkness out of light.

THE WHIPPET BALL

Oh they were happy, their big heads
floating, bloated on vinegar
wine and canned mackerel, music
dancing the wire-rimmed eyeglasses
their guests wore for effect.

From the garden carnations and whippets
blew through the room of white curtains.
The narrow brain-casing
the dogs lived under
carried them to the guests,
out again and back through the kitchen
where the food rested on silver salvers.

The carnations with their clove-fingers
sucked the sky and softened air,
to a four/four rhythm hung
between the lights and the floor.

NEBRASKA CHILDHOOD

They don't have gibbons in Nebraska
This is a sadness of childhood

There are no lions or zebras
to sleep in the pastures

Just a few chicken hawks and groundhogs
run-of-the-mill domestics—cats   dogs

lizards kept in a glass tank
with painted carnival turtles

In the long flatness of the afternoon
little lives to amuse

It is summer
In the autumn

we will build a giraffe out of wood
with a hollow neck and a tube running

the full length   It will drink
calmly from the hummingbird feeder

THE GATHERING

Cigar smoke circulates the room,
the whimps whine to hirsute females—
they might have characters for cousins
or an aunt fond of gelfilte and Wheat Thins,
but they lose anyway. Pintles!

1958. Jimmy Rogers sings soft as the tit
you want off your sister's best friend
home from college in Missouri, full
of accent and the blond scent of swamp root.

The house smells of dill
or chicken fat. Chicago
this time of year is fat with brown.
Your mother pokes you after dinner:
So you can't mingle a little?
Your father adds *mensch*
from the pinochle table.

But later you're lucky, you corner the friend
and talk her up. You plan to meet
in the ping-pong room at three—
your sarcasm wins for you there.

At breakfast over kippers you wipe
the grease off your smirk. You're mean,
the occasion's over and you need something
to look forward to.
You think of the plane trip back:
the stewardess who passes
the chewing gum
before the descent.

BRANDY CAT

Saddened by the aluminum in her
bright eyes, he lets her go wandering back
to a lineage of brandy cats, unsure
of their place on the glass fence. Manners lack
grace when they lick at the meal like fire,
letting hunger rifle the food, but she
makes up for what she lacks there with attire.
Still, a fork lies tarnished by John Dory,
turning dull as coins dipped in mercury
and left overnight. With a sigh the host
pouts onto his Medoc as her hands coast
over the table, clicking his fine silver.
Finally it comes to apples and Brie,
and he ponders the final maneuver.

THE GIRL WHO DOESN'T SMILE

I am seated
in her immaculate salon,
my head cupped in the hand
of her private chair.
When she enters
I see immediately
that her passion is skin deep.
She puts her hand on my chin
and things begin: softly,
she slips her fingers
into my mouth, bending close,
her eyes to my eyes, her eyes
looking away. My elbow
gently rests against her stomach.
We are alone.

It's a strange girl who never smiles,
I think, a little on edge—
her serious face and tools
so pointed. I can see
she's not in this for fun,
yet does
find pleasure somewhere

in the pocket of my mouth.
And her fingers
bring tears to my eyes.

When it's over
she pulls her fingers from me
and I draw in my elbow.
She looks into my eyes at last
and I see there, in her triumph,
the passion that has kept from her
my own undying love.

CLOVE AS EGO

1

Somewhere, farther even than the Sahara,
she is in her pink-and-lime
kitchen, boiling onions in cream.
She is not one for vegetables, yet
turns indifference into the invention
of herself
via simple herbs and spices.
The fingers of her hands find cloves
a sister to the white cream,
the scored balls
within balls.
Here, near the earthenware pot,
we sit with spoons, spoiled
by hunger, the special
acumen of her ego.

2

Inside the porticoes of the state
treasury building, she is
photographed for the slicks.
The flash bulbs find, in a series
of tiny explosions, the crazy-lace
agates that line her fingers.

3
The hot-spice invention of this long-
legged, long-fingered lady
with crazy-lace for nails
and a mouth
tough as a sand bass, stands
between the columns of the treasury,
the indifferent green
bills like tongues licking
through the memory of her pink-
and-lime kitchen, as she cooks onions,
glazed, boiled, or fried with herbs
and the habit of us
with her, watchers, pale salmon in her life
who climb hunger, waiting
upside down, ready to give her
the final attention of our special appetite.

ENDINGS

1

A few years later
(it was on a wet day),
he was killed in an accident
in the streets of Paris.
She was terribly lonely
and looked tired and broken,
but she worked on.

2

His speeches were short and sweet.
One of them ended,
If elected I shall be thankful.
If not, it will be all the same.

3

And yet, none dare openly
love him.
That would have been undue indulgence
and bad for the boy.
So, what with scolding and chiding,
he became very much the stray dog
without a master.

4
He was as much a stranger to the stars
as were his innocent customers,
yet he said things
that pleased and astonished everyone.
The note he left explained,
"That was more a matter of study,
practice, and shrewd guesswork."

5
But now it is different.
I have lost everything.
Death is beautiful.
I will go tired and broken
when I have walked
three thousand times
round this floor.